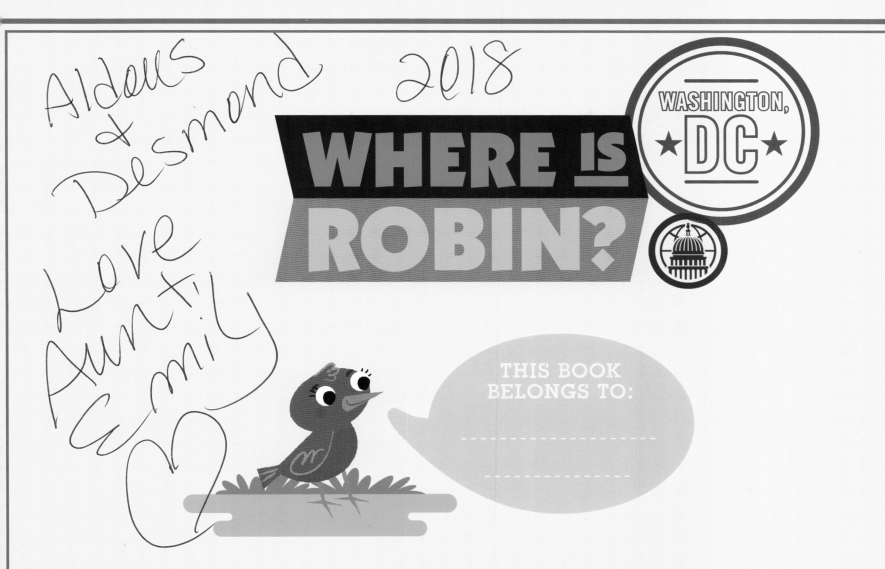

Aldous & Desmond
2018

Love
Aunt Emily

WHERE IS ROBIN?

WASHINGTON, DC

THIS BOOK
BELONGS TO:

....

....

CREATED & WRITTEN BY ROBIN BARONE
ILLUSTRATED BY DANIEL LEE

THIS BOOK IS DEDICATED TO

The travelers who went before me, alongside me, and those yet to come.

ABOUT WHERE IS ROBIN?

We are a platform that uses adventure travel to teach children about the world.

- DREAM - - PLAN - - GO -

Text & art © 2018 Diplomat Books
Text by Robin N. Barone
Illustrations by Daniel Lee
Published in 2018 by Diplomat Books

Typeset in Revers.

Printed in China.

For sales inquiries, contact sales@diplomatbooks.com.

DIPLOMAT BOOKS

Diplomat Books
New York, New York

www.diplomatbooks.com

ISBN 978-0-9906310-6-4

MADE WITH ♥ IN THE USA

Robin's train pulled into Union Station in the capital city.
She was greeted by her friend as her welcoming committee.

Washington, DC is a district and not a state.
In 1790, the U.S. Constitution set the city's fate!

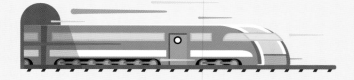

Off to the Capitol, Robin visited her Representative in Congress.
She was curious if the law up for vote had made progress.

"Is the current law you're amending the best version?" she asked.
She imagined that the vote was announced on news broadcast.

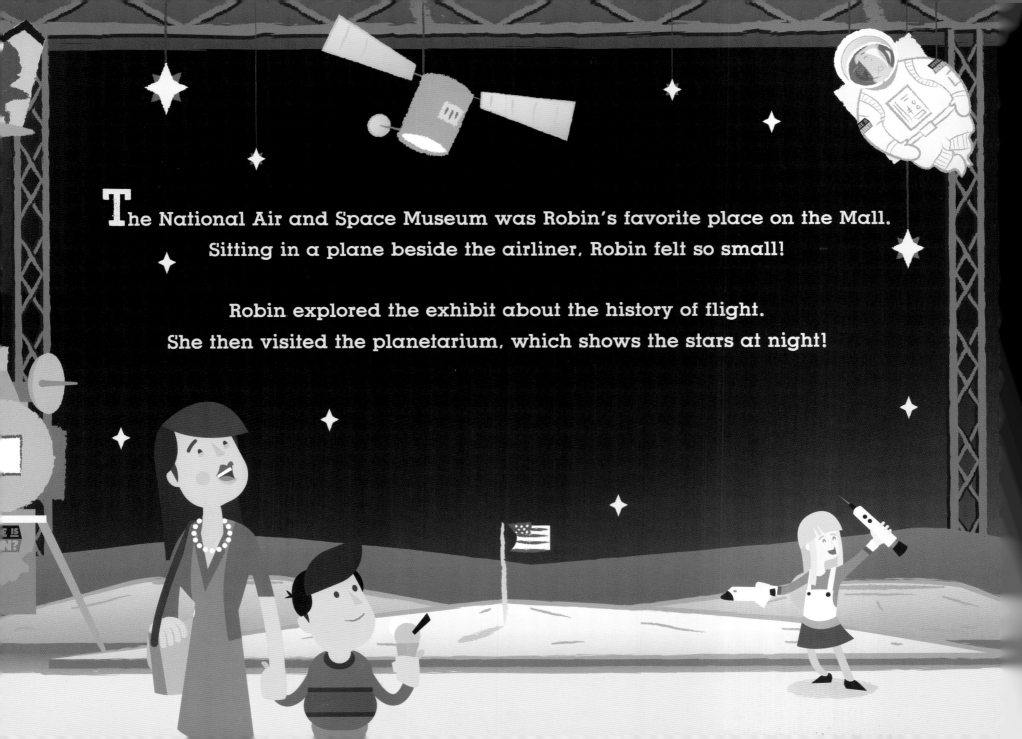

The National Air and Space Museum was Robin's favorite place on the Mall.
Sitting in a plane beside the airliner, Robin felt so small!

Robin explored the exhibit about the history of flight.
She then visited the planetarium, which shows the stars at night!

At the National Press Club, Robin announced her road tour.
"The world has so much to offer. I want to explore!"

Robin stood at the podium and felt free to express.
Her views were protected by the First Amendment's freedom of the press.

At 1600 Pennsylvania Avenue, Robin visited the home of the President.
Sitting in the Oval Office, she felt the power of what the
White House meant.

"One day, I could be the leader of the free world!"
In her mind, the dream of becoming the President swirled.

On the stage of the Howard Theatre, Robin performed as the first act.
She looked out at the crowd. The theater was packed!

This theater for the people was a historic stage.
It was a destination where rock and blues came of age.

POLITICS & PROSE
Dream.Plan.Go
Dream.Plan.Go
Dream.Plan.Go
Dream.Plan.Go

Robin arrived at Dupont Circle in DC's Northwest.
In the center, she found the perfect place to rest.

Around the fountain which was a famous landmark,
musicians played and artists painted in the park.

Walking along Embassy Row, Robin felt the international spirit.
She admired the hanging flags from countries that she wanted to visit.

Embassies are where ambassadors work and live.
They help their countries' foreign affairs be collaborative!

Robin took the subway to Woodley Park to visit the National Zoo,
where she watched the panda from China eat bamboo!

The National Zoo is dedicated to animal conservation.
Without their efforts, many animals would face extinction!

In Georgetown Harbor, Robin boarded a city cruise.
From a boat on the Potomac River, Robin observed the best city views!

Georgetown is a neighborhood full of history.
It is also home to a famous university.

Dream.Plan.Go

At the Kennedy Center, there was a special performance.
Robin joined the principal ballerina for a dance!

On stage, Robin enjoyed her time as a muse.
Could her role be reported on the evening news?

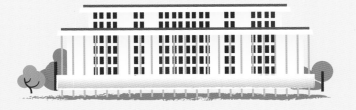

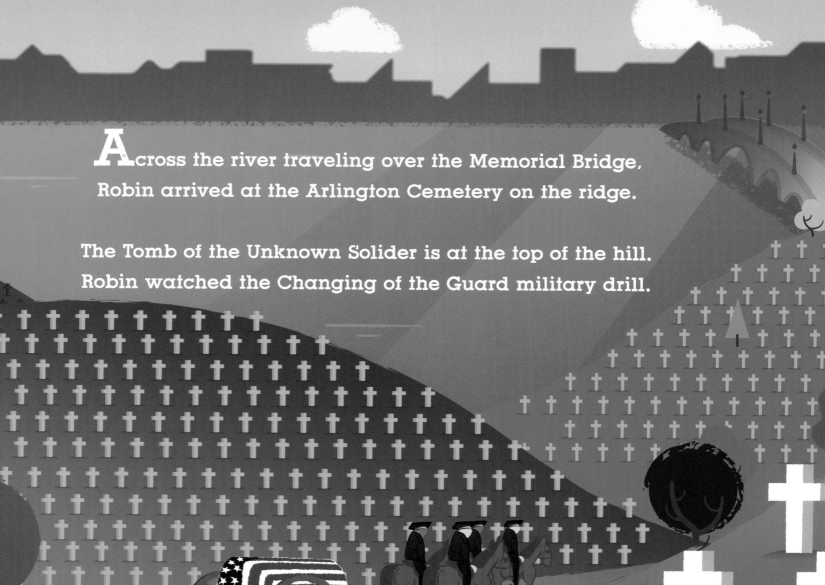

Across the river traveling over the Memorial Bridge,
Robin arrived at the Arlington Cemetery on the ridge.

The Tomb of the Unknown Solider is at the top of the hill.
Robin watched the Changing of the Guard military drill.

At the Lincoln Memorial, Robin stood by the Reflecting Pool.
She learned about the 16th President while she studied in school.

President Lincoln was known for his leadership to end slavery.
This Memorial was built to honor his wisdom and bravery!

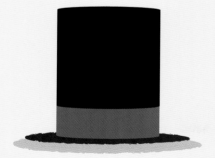

WHERE IS ROBIN?   WHERE IS ROBIN?   WHERE IS ROBIN?

Dream.Plan.Go Dream.Plan.Go Dream.Plan.Go Dream.Plan.Go Dream.Plan.Go Dream.Plan.Go Dream.Plan.Go

At the Vietnam Memorial, Robin laid flowers to remember
soldiers killed in action.
She was surprised to find her eyes tearing and then crying as a reaction.

Robin looked along the wall and saw the reflection of her face.
She placed her wings along the wall and found a solder's name to trace.

Standing in the shadow of the Washington Monument,
Robin reflected on the legacy of the first president.

Located in the center of the Mall,
the obelisk stands 555 feet tall!

Robin headed to the museum dedicated to remembering the Holocaust, where the memory of those who suffered would not be lost.

In the Tower of Faces, Robin paid respect to the people that did not survive. Their portraits on the wall keep their memories alive.

WHERE IS ROBIN?

WHERE IS ROBIN?

WHERE IS RO

THOMAS JEFFERSON
1743–1826

Plan. Go   Dream. Plan. Go   Dream. Plan. Go

Plan. Go   Dream. Plan. Go

Outside of the Jefferson Memorial, the cherry blossoms from Japan bloom.
Inside, a bronze statue of the third President stands alone in the room.

Thomas Jefferson was one of the Declaration of Independence's authors.
He was a diplomat, a statesman, and one of the founding fathers.

The Library of Congress is a national center for learning.
Preserving books and achievements keep visitors returning!

Robin was curious to learn about American history in the Library's collection.
The librarian directed her upstairs to the non-fiction section.

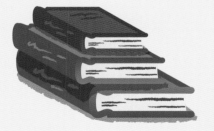

Robin presented her argument to the Justices on the Supreme Court.
Her opinion was argued with tremendous support.

Established in 1789, the Supreme Court is the highest court in the land.
It's the last chance for a plaintiff's defense to take a stand!

In Nationals Park, Robin played in a baseball game.
"The Republicans playing the Democrats! Baseball will never be
the same!"

"My tour is almost over. Soon it will be time to go.
Before I leave, I want to head to the river for a quick row!"

Across the Potomac River and along King Street,
Robin found herself at a place where the past and present meet.

After an amazing day, Robin had dinner in Alexandria's Old Town.
She ended her trip sharing stories as the sun went down.

Follow Robin's other adventures!

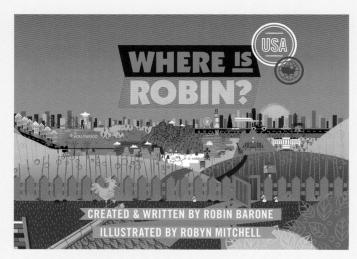

Where is Robin? USA
ISBN: 978-0-9906310-9-5

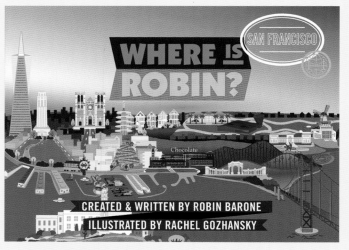

Where is Robin? San Francisco
ISBN: 978-1-946564-06-1

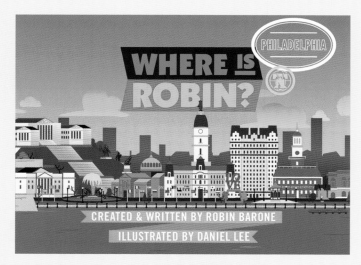

Where is Robin? Philadelphia
ISBN: 978-0-9906310-5-7

Where is Robin? Los Angeles
ISBN: 978-0-9906310-8-8

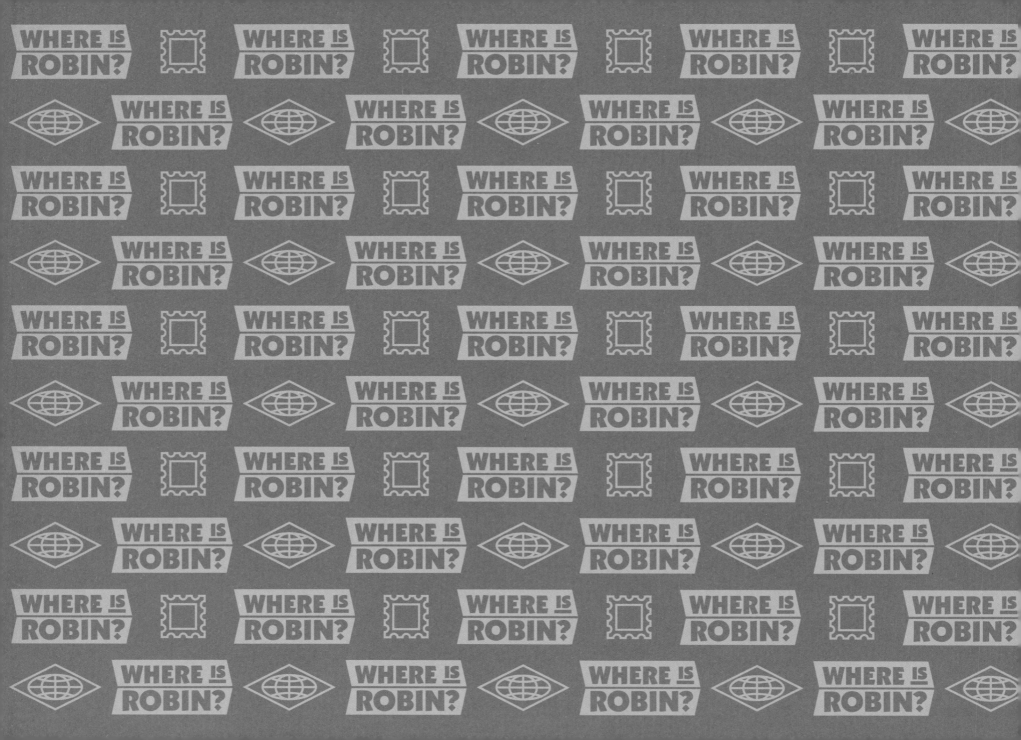